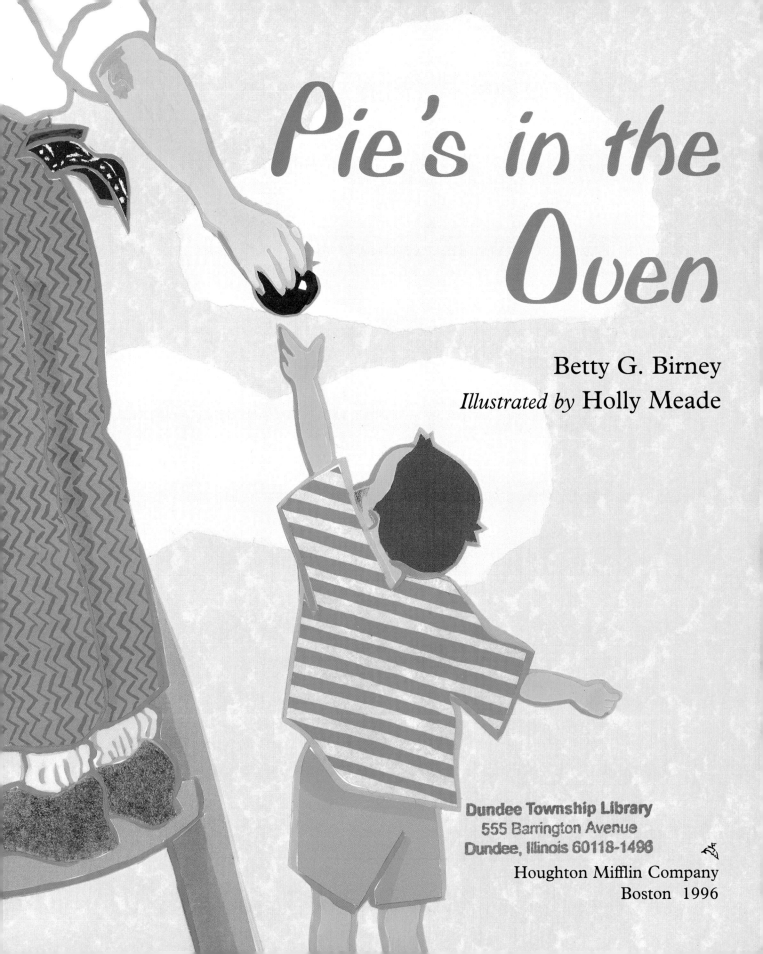

Pie's in the Oven

Betty G. Birney

Illustrated by Holly Meade

Houghton Mifflin Company
Boston 1996

To my sister, Janet

—B.G.B.

*For my father Russell, brother Jeffrey,
and nephew Benjamin, all true
appreciators of homemade pie.*

—H.M.

Text copyright © 1996 by Betty G. Birney
Illustrations copyright © 1996 by Holly Meade

For information about this and other Houghton Mifflin trade
and reference books and multimedia products, visit
The Bookstore at Houghton Mifflin on the World Wide Web
at http://www.hmco.com/trade/.

The text of this book is set in 17.5 Monotype Plantin.
The illustrations are paper collage, reproduced in full color.

Library of Congress Cataloging-in-Publication Data

Birney, Betty G.
Pie's in the oven / by Betty G. Birney ; illustrated by Holly Meade.
p.   cm.
Summary: Because so many people arrive to eat Grandma's pie,
the plate is empty before the little boy gets any, but Grandma
has a surprise in the oven.
ISBN 0-395-76501-3
[1. Pies — Fiction.   2. Grandmothers — Fiction.]
I. Meade, Holly, ill. II. Title.
PZ7.B5229Pi   1996   [E]—dc20
95-43096   CIP   AC

Printed in the United States of America
HOR 10 9 8 7 6 5 4 3 2 1

Grandma has a big surprise.
Pie's in the oven.
I can't wait!

Dry the dishes while it bakes.
Pie's in the oven,
My favorite kind!

"Something smells good," Grandpa says.
Pie's in the oven.
Don't you peek!

Lots of apples, sugar, and spice.
Pie's in the oven,
Bubbly and brown.

Annie's at the fence now, shouting "Yoo-hoo!"

Pie's in the oven.
Better hurry!

Irene's in the garden, hanging up the wash.

Pie's in the oven.
Come right in!

Postman's at the front door — knock-knock-knock!
Pie's in the oven.
Hope you're hungry!

Trixie's at the back door, scratching to get in.
Pie's in the oven.
Mmmmm, smells good!

Fire truck's coming with Grandpa's pals!
Pie's in the oven.
You're just in time.

Now who's coming up the walk?
Lucille, Nora, Babe, and Ed,
Uncle Will and Uncle Fred,

Great-Aunt Minnie, Cousin Ben,
Ray, Marie . . . where will it end?
Pie's in the oven.
Plenty for all!

"Come on, Jenny. Bring a friend!"
Pie's in the oven.
Don't miss out.

Bring those chairs in from the porch.
Pie's in the oven.
Pour the milk.

Pass the plates and get the knife.
Pie's in the oven,
But not for long.

A piece for Annie. Will wants two.
Pie's on the table.
It's my turn soon!

Save a piece for Grandpa's lunch.
Pie's going fast now.
Where's my piece?

Pie plate's empty . . . and so am I!

Pie's all gone now,

And I am mad!

"Don't you worry," Grandma says.

Pie's in the oven —
Just for me!

Everybody's laughing, having fun.
Pie's in my tummy,
And I feel great!